The RUNAWAY PANCAKE

Retold by
Mairi Mackinnon

Illustrated by
Silvia Provantini

Reading Consultant: Alison Kelly
Roehampton University

There was once a family
with seven children, and
they were always hungry.

3

One day, their mother decided to make pancakes for breakfast.

First she mixed flour, eggs and milk.

Then she poured the mix
into a pan to cook. She
tossed the first
pancake, up
in the air
and down
again.

Almost ready
now.

But the pancake
didn't want to be
eaten. It jumped
right out of the pan and
rolled out of the door.

"Come back!" called the children and they all went running after it.

The pancake rolled out of the gate and into the road, faster and faster.

The dog was snoozing in his kennel when the pancake rolled past.

Mmm, a pancake!

"You look good,"
he barked.

"Come here
and let me taste you."

"No!" said the pancake and rolled on, with the dog and all the family chasing behind.

A rabbit in a field saw
the pancake rolling past.

Well, I've
never seen that
before.

"How fast you roll!" he
said. "Can I catch you?"

"No, no!" said the
pancake and rolled on, with
the rabbit, the dog and all
the family chasing behind.

16

A duck on the stream saw
the pancake rolling past.

"Stop, Mr. Pancake!" she called. "Just let me try a tiny piece of you."

"No, no, no!" said the
pancake and rolled on,
with the duck, the rabbit,

20

the dog and all the family
chasing behind.

Faster, faster!

A cat in the farmyard
saw the pancake roll past.

Is it a game?

"Stop! Wait for me!"
she called.

"Catch me if you can,"
said the pancake and rolled
on, with the cat, the duck,
the rabbit, the dog and all
the family chasing behind.

24

I'm delicious but you'll never catch me!

25

A goat in a meadow saw
the pancake roll past.

Mmm,
delicious!

"What a fine-looking pancake," he said. "Do you taste as good as you look?"

27

"Of course!" said the
pancake and rolled on...

28

with the goat, the cat,
the duck, the rabbit, the
dog and all the family
chasing behind.

But you're not
tasting me!

A fox in some bushes saw
the pancake rolling past.

"Oh, Mr. Pancake," he
said. "Why is everyone
chasing you? What
have you done?"

"Can't stop
now," said the pancake...

and it hitched a ride
on a kite to escape the fox.

32

It landed at the edge
of a forest. By the forest
was a pig in a pen.

Now the pig wanted to
eat the pancake too, but he
was too clever to say so.

"What's the hurry,
Mr. Pancake?" he asked.
"Let me walk through the
forest with you. It's a
dangerous place."

The pancake looked into
the forest. Maybe the pig
was right.

"Quickly!" he gasped. "Don't let them catch me!"

"What did
you say?" asked
the pig.

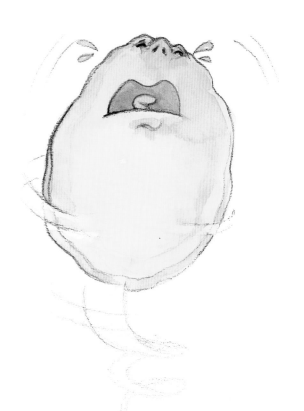

"I SAID, DON'T LET THEM CATCH ME!" shouted the pancake.

"Who?"
asked the pig.
"THEM!" said
the pancake.

42

"I'm sorry," said the pig.
"I can't hear you. You'll
have to come closer."

The pancake jumped over
the fence and into the pen.

"I SAID, THE FOX, THE GOAT," the pancake began. But before he could shout any more, the pig snapped him up and swallowed him...

...in one gulp.

The Runaway Pancake is a folk tale from Germany and Norway. There are different versions with different characters, but the pancake always gets eaten at the end.

Series editor:
Lesley Sims

Designed by
Russell Punter and Louise Flutter

First published in 2006 by Usborne Publishing Ltd., Usborne House, 83-85 Saffron Hill, London EC1N 8RT, England. www.usborne.com
Copyright © 2006 Usborne Publishing Ltd.